Box Turtle

Written and Illustrated by
JOHN HIMMELMAN

we jump in puddles

Guilford, Connecticut

A box turtle is born.

The turtle roams the forest, growing large on leaves, insects, and mushrooms.

In the summer of 1897,
she lays eggs of her own.

The following summer, the turtle walks along
a dirt road. A newly built house sits at the end.

Over the years, more houses appear along the road.

1909. It is a warm summer evening. The turtle catches moths attracted to an electric street lamp.

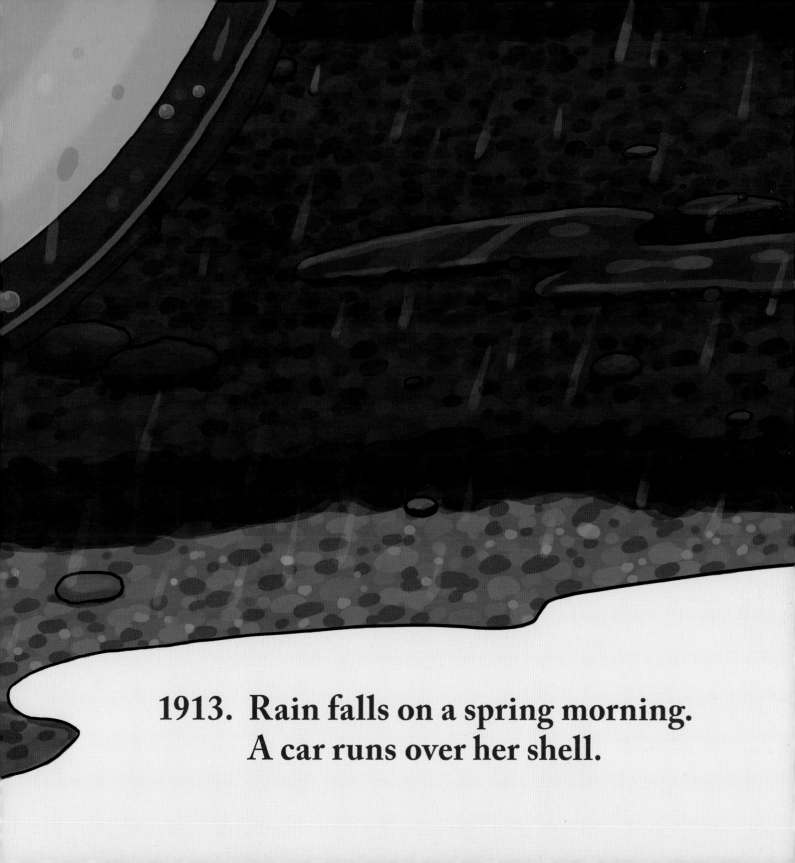

1913. Rain falls on a spring morning.
A car runs over her shell.

The shell is chipped, but she is not hurt.

Fifteen years pass. A boy from one of the houses brings the turtle home as a pet.

The young man graduates high school in 1932. He brings her back to the woods before heading off to college.

**1935. The turtle hears a roar
in the air and looks up.**

Twenty more years pass. More roads now cut through her woods. Houses surround her.

1952. On a quiet autumn morning, the turtle shares a meal with her granddaughter. She turned sixty a month ago. It is the first time they have seen each other.

They both move on.

Protected
Open Space

1986. A new sign is tacked to a tree.
People walk through her woods.

1992. Happy 100th birthday!
A plane flies overhead in a twilight sky.
The turtle does not look up.
She is used to the noise.

2005. A cat paws at her shell.

The turtle has seen many cats and
dogs come and go. She hides in her
shell until the cat moves off.

The turtle's home has grown wild again.
She can barely see the homes around her.

2008. An old man comes across the old turtle. It looks familiar to him. "Were you my pet so many years ago?" he asks.

About Our Turtle

The turtle in this story is an Eastern Box Turtle (Terrapene carolina carolina). While most live 30 to 40 years in the wild, some can live over 100 years. The oldest one is believed to be 145 years old! As with the turtle in this story, it would have been around when the now extinct Passenger Pigeons (seen on the first two pages) were still with us. They have watched in silence the world change around them.

Unlike many of its turtle cousins found in ponds, lakes, and the sea, box turtles live on land. They prefer damp woods of deciduous (broad leaved) trees, where they hunt the forest floor for a variety of food: insects, mushrooms, berries, and other plants and crawly things. They LOVE slugs!

While our box turtle spent some time as someone's pet, they should NEVER be taken from the wild! In some states, like Connecticut, where this turtle's story takes place, removing a box turtle from the wild is a crime. (It wasn't a crime when this story took place, and they were often kept as pets) It is difficult to keep these long-living creatures happy and healthy outside of their native habitat. They deserve to live in their own world.

If you come across a box turtle, enjoy it by taking pictures, or making drawings. It is a good idea to get an image of the plastron (shell on its belly). All individuals have a different pattern and if you come across another turtle over the years, you can see if it's the same one. They are growing more rare throughout their range, so finding one is a cause for excitement!

Should you come upon an injured turtle, contact your state's Department of Environmental Protection. They are likely to know people with the experience and license to help it.

Dedication

For Bruce Dodson, who has spent decades keeping
the forests and fields of our little town of
Killingworth, Connecticut, from disappearing.

An imprint of Globe Pequot

Distributed by NATIONAL BOOK NETWORK

Copyright © 2018 John Himmelman
Cover and interior design by Diana Nuhn

British Library Cataloguing in Publication Information Available
Library of Congress Control Number: 2017918498

ISBN 978-1-63076-331-2 (hardcover)
ISBN 978-1-63076-332-9 (e-book)

Printed in Yuanzhou, China—April 2018